This Is Our Normal

By
Tania Glenn
PsyD, LCSW, CCTP

Illustrations by Kalpart

Progressive
RISING PHOENIX PRESS ®

Text Copyright © 2021 Tania Glenn
All rights reserved.

Published 2021 by
Progressive Rising Phoenix Press, LLC
www.progressiverisingphoenix.com

ISBN: 978-1-950560-56-1

Printed in the U.S.A.

Editor: Jody Amato

Author Photographs (Back Cover & Interior): "Tania Glenn" by Jill Hays, (www.jillhaysphotography.com). Used by permission of the photographer. © Copyright 2020 Jill Hays.

Book Design/Layout, Illustrations and Book Cover design by Kalpart. Visit www.kalpart.com

To Public Safety Children

My name is Christopher, but my friends call me Chris. I am eight years old, and I love to play sports. My family and I spend a lot of time together. We like to go for long bike rides, play games, and roast marshmallows around a fire.

My mom is a nurse, and

my dad is a police officer.

This past year, I went to counseling to help me cope with my worries about my dad.

The tools that Mr. Curtis and his therapy dog, Tyra, taught me have helped me cope with my most recent worries about my mom as well. This has been a rough year for both my mom and my dad.

One day at school, I saw a boy on the playground. He was new, and he looked incredibly sad. Somehow, I just knew I could relate to him, so I asked him his name and why he was so sad.

He told me his name was Marcus and that his dad was in the Army. He was sad because his dad had just left for a year to deploy with the military.

I sat next to Marcus at lunch that day. I learned from counseling that the more we express how we feel, the better we begin to feel. I asked Marcus to tell me about his dad and his life with his family. I mostly just listened.

As we finished lunch, I told Marcus about my recent worries about my family. Marcus looked so relieved. He told me that he felt just like I did.

I shared some of the things I had learned in counseling from Mr. Curtis. Marcus was very thankful.

The next day, Marcus and I sat together at lunch again. We just seemed to understand each other, so we decided to have lunch together every day.

One day, when we were talking, we noticed a girl at the table next to us. She was trying not to cry, and it looked like she was having a terrible day.

We asked her to have lunch with us, so she did. She told us her name was Taylor, but she did not say much else that day, so Marcus and I mostly tried to cheer her up with funny stories about our lives.

18

The next day at lunch, Taylor sat with us again, and this time she was able to open up some more. Taylor told us that her dad was a firefighter and he had been hurt in a fire. She told us that he was going to be ok, but that her home life was very chaotic. Her mom was scared, her dad was hurt, and she just did not know what to do.

Marcus and I listened to her. I shared my experiences in counseling with Mr. Curtis and told her that counseling might help her as well. Taylor began to smile when I told her about Tyra the therapy dog.

The next day at school, Taylor told us her mom had made an appointment for her to go to counseling.

While we were talking, another girl named Isabella overheard us and joined us. Isabella told us that her mom was a flight nurse and that she had heard her parents talking about a fire. Isabella's mom had flown Taylor's dad to the hospital!

22

Suddenly Isabella and Taylor hugged each other. Taylor could not stop telling Isabella how thankful she was for her mom.

Isabella shared with us that a year ago, there was a helicopter crash in a city close by, and that she had had a tough time afterwards. She told us that she worried about her mom every time she went to work. "That's exactly how I feel!" exclaimed Taylor.

At that moment, we all seemed to realize that we were a group of kids with a cool story. Our parents—all first responders and military members—serve and protect others. As their children, we are part of this journey. What connects us are the same worries and fears, but also what connects us is the same pride we have in being a part of helping other people.

The day Taylor had her counseling appointment, she told us during lunch that she was nervous. She mentioned she might not want to go, but all of us encouraged her to try it.

Taylor came to school the next day and was excited to tell us about her counselor, Miss Maggie, who also had a therapy dog, named Arya. She told us that Arya was a big dog who rested her head on Taylor's lap and stared into her eyes the whole time. Taylor told us that Miss Maggie taught her where feelings come from and that they are normal. Miss Maggie gave Taylor some tools to use to manage her feelings when she was sad or stressed.

As we finished lunch that day, I asked Marcus, Taylor, and Isabella to make a toast with our milk. I see my parents do this on special occasions, and I think it's fun to make a toast. As we toasted, I said, "To the first responder kids." Everyone shouted, "To the first responder kids!" Marcus laughed and said, "We may not be like other families, but this is our normal!"

Dear Parents,

The past few years have been especially tough for first responders, and the impact on the families has been significant. I hope you have found this book helpful in starting discussions with your children. Allowing children to express their emotions both through words and play can help alleviate some of the worries they may have.

The children of first responders grow up differently than most kids. Your children learn and experience the selfless care for others and a sense of duty and obligation to your communities that many kids never come to realize. Your kids are resilient and wise. The fact that so many first responders' kids follow in the footsteps of their parents is a true testament to the way they are raised.

Please know that it is ok to reach out for help. Talking to your children, attending therapy, participating in family days at your departments, connecting with other public safety families, and getting educated on stress and trauma are all ways to alleviate the negative impact of the job on the family.

I cannot thank you enough for the sacrifices you make every day. You are loved.

In Gratitude,
Tania Glenn

About the Author

Tania was three months from completing her Master's Degree at the University of Texas when she witnessed the dramatic and violent standoff between law enforcement and the Branch Davidian Cult in Waco, Texas. At that point, she knew her calling was to work with first responders and to focus on healing these warriors from the horrors of post-traumatic stress disorder. Tania spent the first ten years of her career working in a Level Two Trauma Emergency Department on weekend nights as she built her private practice during the week. In 2002, Tania transitioned to her private practice on a full-time basis and has dedicated her entire career to working with first responders and military members. Tania assisted with the aftermath of the Oklahoma City Murrah Federal Building bombing, the 9/11 attacks on the World Trade Center, Hurricane Katrina, the Dallas Police shootings, and numerous other incidents. Tania is referred to as the "warrior healer" by her colleagues, and she is passionate about her work. Tania resides in Central Texas. Her loves include her family, her pets and fitness.

Also by Tania Glenn:

First Responder Resilience: Caring for Public Servants

Code Four: Surviving and Thriving in Public Safety

First Responder Families: Caring for the Hidden Heroes

Smashing The Stigma and Changing the Culture in Emergency Services

I've Got Your 6: Peer Support for First Responders

Protected But Scared
(a book for the children of police officers)

Progressive Rising Phoenix Press is an independent publisher. We offer wholesale discounts and multiple binding options with no minimum purchases for schools, libraries, book clubs, and retail vendors. We also off er rewards for libraries, schools, independent book stores, and book clubs. Please visit our website to see our updated catalogue of titles and our wholesale discount page at: www.ProgressiveRisingPhoenix.com

CPSIA information can be obtained
at www.ICGtesting.com
Printed in the USA
BVHW061711300421
606208BV00002B/42